Shawn Kemp

Additional Titles in the Sports Reports *Series*

Shawn Kemp
Star Forward

Stew Thornley

Enslow Publishers, Inc.

44 Fadem Road	PO Box 38
Box 699	Aldershot
Springfield, NJ 07081	Hants GU12 6BP
USA	UK

Library of Congress Cataloging-in-Publication Data

Thornley, Stew.
     Shawn Kemp: star forward / Stew Thornley.
        p. cm. — (Sports reports)
     Includes bibliographical references (p.) and index.
     Summary: A biography of the Seattle Supersonics' basketball player whose
exciting style of play includes a thundering slam dunk.
     ISBN 0-89490-929-0
     1. Kemp, Shawn—Juvenile literature. 2. Basketball players—United States—
Biography—Juvenile literature. [1. Kemp, Shawn. 2. Basketball players.
3. Afro-Americans—Biography.] I. Title II. Series.
GV884.K45T58   1998
796.332'092—dc21
[B]   96-50050
                                          CIP
                                          AC

Printed in the United States of America

10 9 8 7 6 5 4 3 2 1

Photo Credits: Brian Drake, 1996, pp. 11, 31, 35, 39, 41, 45, 58, 64, 73, 77;
Courtesy of Sioux Falls Skyforce, p. 9; Dennis Anderson, p. 80; George R.
Rekela, pp. 13, 20, 52, 60, 72, 82, 90; John Kovach, p. 25; University of
Nevada-Las Vegas, pp. 17, 49.

Cover Credit: Brian Drake, 1996.

Contents

Chapter 1

Reaching New Heights

The Seattle SuperSonics were on the road for the opening of the 1992–1993 National Basketball Association (NBA) season. This was no ordinary road trip, though. The team would play its first two games of the year in Yokohama, Japan.

Two years before, the NBA had played regular-season games in Tokyo to see how much interest the people of Japan had in the game. The games were so popular that the league decided to do it again.

For Shawn Kemp this game should have been his first in the NBA. If he had completed four years of college, as many players did, he would have been a rookie in 1992. But Kemp never played in college. He had planned on it, but things did not work out that way. One year out of high school, in 1989, Kemp entered the NBA.

Now, in 1992, many players whom Kemp had grown up playing against were finally coming into the league. While players like Alonzo Mourning, Christian Laettner, and Don MacLean were making their NBA debuts that night, Kemp was starting his fourth NBA season.

Only twenty-two players before him had played in the NBA without ever having played a single game in college. Of these, Darryl Dawkins was one of the most well known. Moses Malone, another NBA player who entered professional basketball straight out of high school, played first in the American Basketball Association (ABA), and then in the NBA after the two leagues merged in 1976.

K. C. Jones, who had coached the SuperSonics from 1990 to early 1992, was among those who saw better things in store for Kemp. "The thing Shawn has going for him along with his skills is his love for the game and his work ethic. You can't teach those things. That's at the core of what will make him a great player."[1]

Jones added, "A player with limited talent who works hard can be a good player. A player with a lot of talent who works hard should reach greatness. That's what will take Shawn to the next level."[2] Kemp was

Darryl Dawkins is shown here as a member of the Sioux Falls Skyforce of the Continental Basketball Association (CBA). Known for his backboard shattering slams, Darryl Dawkins was one of the few players who went into the NBA directly after high school.

reaching the next level as the 1992–1993 season began. He was best known for his thunderous dunk shots.

The fans especially hoped to see an alley-oop dunk. An alley-oop play consists of a player lobbing a high pass toward the basket. A teammate will jump to grab the ball, and while still in the air, slam it through the basket. The play requires great timing and teamwork.

Kemp, however, could do more than dunk. He was refining his game in other ways. He played the position of power forward. Unlike the other forward spot (often called "small forward"), the role of the power forward is not to rack up high point totals. Power forwards are called upon to rebound, grab missed shots, and keep rallies alive for their team.

One standard of success for a power forward is to have a "double-double" in a game, which means reaching double figures (ten or more) in any two of the following: scoring, rebounding, blocked shots, or assists.

Kemp hoped to get the 1992–1993 season off to a good start with a double-double. Yokohama Arena was packed for the game between the SuperSonics and Houston Rockets. Not only were all the seats filled, more than two thousand standing-room-only tickets had also been sold.

Kemp was aware of how much the fans enjoyed his style of play, and he did what he could

FACT

Besides Moses Malone, and Darryl Dawkins, only twenty other players had made it to the NBA without ever playing in college before Shawn Kemp joined the Seattle SuperSonics in 1989. Those players are Norm Baker, Stan Brown, Jim Browne, Al Cervi, Herm Fuetsch, Wilfred (Pop) Goodwin, Leo (Ace) Gottlieb, Joe Graboski, Reggie Harding, Matthew (Nat) Hickey, Tony Kappen, Bob Knight, Stan Miasek, Red Mihalik, John Murphy, Nick Shaback, Connie Simmons, Ed Stanczak, Isaac (Rabbit) Walthour, and Bill Willoughby.

Defying gravity, Shawn Kemp throws down another slam dunk.

to give them what they wanted. "The style we play is fast-break and exciting, and that's what the crowd likes to see," he said after the game. "They like to see different people doing different things, like my dunks."[3]

An alley-oop play put the SuperSonics ahead in the game, 44–29. The Rockets came back strong in the second half, though. Early in the fourth quarter Houston held an 85–80 lead. Nate McMillan and Kemp sparked a rally. Instead of a dunk, though, Kemp went with a soft touch. He converted a reverse layup after taking a pass from McMillan. This started a nine-point run that put the Sonics ahead to stay.

Kemp scored 29 points in the game to help Seattle win, 111–94. One of the keys to victory was dominant rebounding. Houston rarely got second chances at baskets as the Sonics' front line gobbled up missed Rocket shots. Kemp himself finished with 20 rebounds.

The Sonics and Rockets played to another sold-out crowd the next night. Seattle won again, this time by a score of 89–85. Kemp had another double-double with 20 points and 12 rebounds. It was exactly the kind of start the SuperSonics were hoping for, both for the team and for Shawn Kemp.

These kinds of performances made it easy for

some people, including Kemp, to forget that he was still a few weeks short of his twenty-second birthday. "When I step on the court, I don't feel young at all," he said, "and it doesn't seem like anyone treats me that way, either."[4]

His coaches did not treat him like a kid, although they knew Kemp was still improving and could look forward to even greater achievements. "So much of his progress and growth is just the experience of playing," said SuperSonics' head coach George Karl. "It's exciting to be part of his growth."[5]

As for Kemp, he was not going to be satisfied until he reached the top. "Being the best is what I shoot for," he said as the 1992–1993 season opened. "When I'm on the court, I want respect from the other players. I want them to think, 'If he's not one of the best, he's right up there with the best.'"[6]

George Karl took over as head coach of the Seattle SuperSonics during the 1991–1992 season, and since then has led the team into the NBA Finals.

Chapter 2

Michiana

The northern portion of Indiana—a strip that borders the state line with Michigan—is informally known as Michiana. Although it is almost considered part-Indiana, part-Michigan, it is all Indiana as far as attitudes toward basketball are concerned. "Basketball may have been invented in Massachusetts," said Bobby Knight, the legendary coach at Indiana University, "but it was made for Indiana."[1] Basketball is taken seriously in all parts of the state, including Michiana. Throughout Elkhart County in the heart of Michiana, a basketball hoop is attached to nearly every garage.

In the city of Elkhart, Barbara Kemp was raising her two children in the 1970s. A single parent,

Barbara worked in the records department of a hospital. She worked hard but still found time to spend with her daughter Lisa, and Lisa's younger brother Shawn.

Shawn was talented in a variety of sports. In baseball he could deliver a burning fastball, although without much control. He could also fling a football a long distance. Certainly, though, he was most gifted at basketball. From the time he was four years old, he was constantly bouncing or shooting a basketball and developing the talent that would someday make him a star.

As he grew up, Kemp was always the biggest kid in his class, and he was definitely the best at basketball. Eventually he began competing in youth tournaments all over the United States. Here he had the chance to play with and against some of the best young players in the country. Billy Owens and Alonzo Mourning were two players who participated in these tournaments and also went on to play in the NBA.

In taking part in these events Kemp came to the attention of college coaches. One of them was Tim Grgurich, who was an assistant coach at the University of Nevada-Las Vegas (UNLV) when Kemp competed in a Las Vegas tournament in 1984. "He was . . . the best player we had ever seen," said

FACT

Shawn was not the only member of the Kemp family with athletic talent. His older sister Lisa was also a talented basketball player. The two of them often matched up in one-on-one games. It was not until Shawn became a teenager that he could handle his sister on the court.

Tim Grgurich, then an assistant coach at the University of Nevada-Las Vegas, noticed Kemp while Kemp was still competing in youth tournaments. Grgurich knew then that Kemp would become a pro player.

Grgurich. "We were saying then that the kid was going to be a pro. . . . He was special."[2]

A few years later Grgurich tried to recruit Kemp for UNLV. He was not successful. Eventually, though, Grgurich did get the chance to coach Kemp in the NBA when he became an assistant coach with the SuperSonics.

It was while he was playing in national tournaments that Kemp started to dunk the ball. After a missed shot by one of his teammates, Kemp jumped into the air and grabbed the rebound. In the same motion, he stuffed it back through the basket.

He learned two things from the experience. One was that a dunk was the most accurate shot a player could make. The other was that a dunk could be a spectacular play that would light up the crowd. These lessons stayed with Kemp when he got back to Elkhart. On the playgrounds he loved to jam the ball through the hoop as hard as he could. Many of the baskets on these outdoor courts have chain-link nets. Sometimes he could dunk the ball with enough force to create sparks.

He often ended up with bruises and cuts on his wrists from banging against the rim. But he would not stop. "When I dunk, I just want to tear the rim down," he said.[3]

By this time, Shawn Kemp was playing on the varsity team at Concord High School. He was also going through another growth spurt that put him close to his present six-foot ten-inch height.

His coach on the Concord Minutemen was Jim Hahn. The Minutemen won only six of nineteen games in Hahn's first season at Concord. The next year Shawn Kemp joined the team as a ninth-grader.

During one of the team's first practices, Kemp and Hahn had a disagreement on how Kemp would play offense. Hahn pointed to the door and let Kemp know he could leave if he did not want to do it Hahn's way. Kemp left.

Hahn was terrified he had just lost the player he was counting on to help the Minutemen improve. A few minutes later Kemp returned. "I wasn't mad," Kemp explained. "Growing up, I was always able to play the way I wanted to play and do what I wanted to do. It had never been put across to me that way before. I just went out to collect my thoughts."[4]

From then on the coach and budding star got along well. Hahn helped Kemp develop into a well-rounded player. He taught him a lot about blocking shots on defense as well as passing the ball and shooting on offense. Even after he made it in the NBA, Kemp had good words to say about Hahn. "Jim was a good coach, and he also was a teacher

Shawn Kemp attended Concord High School. He made the varsity basketball team as a freshman.

and father to me. He was the guy who would stay on me when . . . I would be lackadaisical."[5]

Concord became a much better team with Kemp's help. The Minutemen won their sectional tournament when Kemp was a freshman. The next year they made it a step further, winning the regional title and advancing to the state semi-finals.

While starring at Concord and competing in national tournaments, Kemp started to realize how good he was and started thinking about a pro career in basketball.

Unfortunately he did not do as well in the classroom as he did on the basketball court. He did not approach his studies with the same effort he put into basketball. He kept his grades high enough to stay eligible for sports, but his inattention to schoolwork would eventually catch up with him.

There was also another difficult challenge for Kemp to contend with. Most of the students in his school were white, as were the students in most of the schools Concord played against. Kemp was usually one of the few black players on the court when he played. When Concord played on the road, the fans sometimes taunted Kemp with racial slurs.

Somehow Kemp kept his composure through all of this. His coach claimed that it caused him to play even better. "He was able to use the taunts to his advantage," said Hahn. "He wouldn't lash out or retaliate, even though it bothered him a lot. He got back at his critics by beating them."[6]

There would be other problems for Kemp to deal with. Before his senior season, he announced his choice of a college. The state of Indiana has several schools with outstanding basketball programs: Purdue, Indiana University, and Notre Dame, which is barely over thirty miles away from Elkhart, are among them. Kemp chose none of these. He decided to go to a college in a different state.

This did not sit well with many Indiana residents. They became even more upset when Kemp announced that the college he was going to was the University of Kentucky. Kentucky bordered Indiana to the south and was Indiana's chief rival for basketball dominance.

Fans at opposing schools gave Kemp an even harder time since they felt that he was being disloyal to Indiana by choosing the Kentucky Wildcats. Before long they had additional ammunition with which to taunt Kemp.

Academically Kemp failed to meet the minimum score on his college Scholastic Aptitude Test (SAT). This meant that he would be ineligible to play as a college freshman. When word of his score got out, the racial slurs turned to jabs at his intelligence. Fans from opposing schools would chant, "S-A-T . . . S-A-T." Concord fans would scream back, "N-B-A . . . N-B-A," to remind others that Kemp would someday be a star in the National Basketball Association.

The Minutemen, meanwhile, had a marvelous season during Kemp's senior year. They were undefeated and made it all the way to the state championship game before losing. The jeers and insults that Kemp received, however, made it a difficult year for him. Ben Barnes, a member of the Elkhart County Council and a leader in the African-American community, said Kemp handled the situation as well as anyone could have: "If Shawn did one thing well as a youngster it was that he held his composure," said Barnes. "It was pretty hard on all of us, having to listen to some of the things people were saying."[7]

Another disappointment for Kemp came when the Indiana Mr. Basketball voting was announced. He did not receive the award, which had been his goal ever since he was in eighth grade. Many people felt that he was the most deserving, but, that he was cast aside by voters who were upset that he had chosen to attend college in Kentucky.

Kemp was a hero at Concord though. The Minutemen had a win-loss record of 85–19 in his four years there. After he graduated, Concord

FACT

Because basketball is so popular in Indiana, many of the state's high-school gyms are huge. The Concord gym could fit nearly three thousand fans. That was not big enough, however, once Kemp started playing for the Minutemen. Eventually the school knocked out one end of the gym so that another eight hundred seats could be put in. This expanded area is still known as "Kemp's Addition."

retired his number 40. No Minutemen player has ever worn that number since.

Kemp was considered the best of a high school class that included Alonzo Mourning of Indian River High School in Chesapeake, Virginia; Billy Owens of Carlisle High School in Pennsylvania; and Chris Jackson, who later changed his name to Mahmoud Abdul-Rauf, of Gulfport High School in Mississippi.

Kemp would not be playing basketball his freshman year in college, however. "It was my own fault for ignoring academics. I'm not dumb; I'm not stupid. But I just didn't push myself," said Kemp. He also ridiculed those who said Proposition 48, which made him ineligible to play, was unfair. "I don't have any problems with it. It's fair. The only person who held me back was myself."[8] Proposition 48 meant that Kemp would not be eligible to play basketball during his freshman year, due to his low SAT scores.

Going to college but not being able to play basketball would be difficult for Kemp. Hahn even urged Kemp not to do it and to consider playing basketball in Europe for a year before coming to Kentucky. "Every single athlete is not meant for college," Hahn said later. "To have Shawn in a college environment without basketball, the one thing he loves, was, I felt, a big mistake. It even crossed my mind to advise him to go right into the NBA, and

Concord High School retired Kemp's number (40). The display case at Concord High shows some of the highlights of Kemp's basketball career.

the only thing that stopped me was the fact that so few players have done it."[9]

Almost all American players who have gone into the NBA have played some college basketball. College is a place to refine skills before joining the professional ranks. Kemp planned to stay at Kentucky and begin playing basketball his second year there.

At the time Kemp decided to attend Kentucky, however, the school was in the midst of problems with the National Collegiate Athletic Association (NCAA). The NCAA had accused the Wildcats of paying players, which was a violation of amateur rules. Kemp expected this issue to be cleared up by the time he started at Kentucky. Instead, new problems surfaced. There was a major scandal over money that the school was said to have sent to the father of one of its star recruits. It became apparent that the school would be placed on probation by the NCAA. This could mean that the Wildcats would not be eligible for post-season play and would not appear on national television.

Kemp was not involved in any wrongdoing himself, but he would suffer the effects of the team's probation by the time he was eligible to play. As a result, he decided to go elsewhere.

In November of his freshman year, Kemp transferred to Trinity Valley Community College in

Athens, Texas. He still would not be able to play basketball until the next season, but at least he was able to work out with the team.

In spring 1989, however, Kemp made a decision. Instead of waiting to play basketball the following season for Trinity Valley, he would make himself eligible for the NBA draft.

Kemp visited cities of a number of NBA teams for interviews and workouts. In Seattle the SuperSonics put him through a series of physical tests and seemed impressed with him. On draft day the Sonics pulled off a trade that gave them two consecutive selections in the first round. The team's greatest need was for a point guard. It took care of that by drafting Dana Barros out of Boston College. With its next pick, the team took Kemp.

Kemp was the seventeenth player selected overall in the draft. Some people felt the SuperSonics were taking a chance by drafting someone who had not played in college. The SuperSonics, however, felt that Kemp was good enough to take that chance.

Kemp's high school coach was delighted to see him selected so high in the draft. He remembered the abuse Kemp had taken in high school and hoped that this would be a way to get it behind him. "I want Shawn to do well so he'll silence his critics," said Hahn. "I want Shawn to have the last word."[10]

Chapter 3

Starting Out in Seattle

In autumn 1989 Shawn Kemp arrived at his first day of training camp with the Seattle SuperSonics and made it known that, "I didn't come here to sit on the bench."[1]

The coaching staff had other ideas, however. Head coach Bernie Bickerstaff had a plan for Kemp. He would bring him along slowly and give him a chance to adjust. Some of the players who he would be facing had more than fifteen years of experience in the league.

Bickerstaff knew that Kemp had tremendous skills. Yet he never had the chance to polish some of his rough edges in college. No doubt he would smooth out his game playing against the best the league had to offer. It would not be wise, however, to let Kemp try to work out the kinks all at once.

Kemp was only nineteen years old. He was the youngest player in the National Basketball Association. In addition to developing as a basketball player, he needed to develop as a person. Bickerstaff, along with assistants Bob Kloppenburg and Tom Newell, were more than just coaches to Kemp. They watched out for him in a fatherly sort of way. It was a different type of situation for everyone on the SuperSonics to handle, but it was not difficult. Kemp fit right in and was popular with his teammates right from the start.

Kemp's best friend on the team was Dana Barros, the player who had been selected just ahead of him in the college draft. Even though Barros was more than two-and-a-half years older, they were both rookies. They had each other to lean on as they entered professional basketball together.

The SuperSonics' first game of the 1989–1990 season was against a team playing its first regular-season game ever—the Minnesota Timberwolves. New teams were not expected to do very well, but the Minnesota team gave the SuperSonics all they could handle. Finally, though, Seattle took charge.

With the game in control, Coach Bickerstaff thought that the time was right for Kemp to get his

Shawn Kemp teaches Cliff Robinson of the Portland Trail Blazers that it is not a good idea to get in the way when Kemp is trying to score.

start. If Kemp was nervous when he stepped on the court for his first NBA game, he did not show it. In the ten minutes that he played, he took three shots from the field. Only one went in, but he showed he was not afraid to shoot the ball. He added a free throw and finished the game with 3 points. He also pulled down 3 rebounds in his brief appearance in the game.

In the Sonics' next game, Kemp got even more playing time, and he responded by scoring 8 points. Bickerstaff was careful to pick the right time to put Kemp into games. He wanted Kemp to build his confidence, but not when the outcome of the game was on the line.

Gradually his minutes played, along with his spirit, increased. It was all a part of growing, of working his way into the league.

Kemp knew that his chance would come. When it did, he would make the most of it. He did just that less than two weeks into the season in a game at the Seattle Center Coliseum against the Washington Bullets. Kemp scored 18 points in just twenty minutes of play. He also collected 9 rebounds and played some tough defense, blocking 3 shots.

Late in the game, Kemp turned on the burners. He scored by tipping in a teammate's missed shot.

Down at the other end of the court, he then blocked a shot by Melvin Turpin. As Turpin went sprawling into the front rows of seats, Kemp and the Sonics raced back down court. Dana Barros lofted a pass toward the rim and Kemp broke toward the basket. Kemp grabbed the pass and stuffed it through the hoop. The crowd went wild as the two Seattle newcomers combined on a beautiful alley-oop play.

It was easy for people to forget that one of those newcomers was still a teenager. Kemp's great performance against the Bullets came ten days before his twentieth birthday. He showed his youthful inexperience in a number of ways. One was his tendency to strut a bit after a thundering dunk shot. His antics sometimes irritated opponents, but the Seattle fans ate it up.

Even though his playing time was still limited, Kemp was emerging as Seattle's most electrifying player. He was also becoming active in the community. "This city is starving for a personality, and Shawn has a chance to be it," said Jim Marsh, the director of community relations for the SuperSonics. "He's done more in the community in the few weeks he's been here than a lot of players have done over their whole careers. "He could have Seattle in the palm of his hand."[2]

Kemp was more than an exciting player for the SuperSonics, he was also versatile. During his rookie season he played all three front-court positions: small forward, power forward, and center. His ability to step in and play a variety of positions allowed his teammates to get some much-needed breaks during the games. In return, Kemp learned from his teammates, including Xavier McDaniel:

> X [Xavier McDaniel] really taught me a lot about the way you have to handle yourself on the basketball floor. He told me right off not to take anything from anybody, or they'll keep giving it to you. All I could do my first year was to make sure nobody outworked me. I just gave it everything I had full speed. Sometimes that was good, and sometimes that was bad.[3]

Kemp did not always come out on top, but he enjoyed every chance he had to go up against the more established players.

> I was trying to make them work on defense. To stop great players, you have to take it back to them. . . . In this league, to prove you're a real player, you have to play well against [the great ones.][4]

Kemp's longest playing time in a game came during the 1989–1990 season, on January 20 in Phoenix, Arizona, in a game against the Suns. He

FACT

As a rookie, Kemp had the chance to showcase his skills on All-Star Weekend in Miami. He competed in the annual Slam Dunk Championship the day before the All-Star Game. San Antonio's David Robinson and Utah's Blue Edwards were the only other rookies taking part in All-Star activities that weekend. Kemp finished fourth in the contest.

Shawn Kemp grabs the loose ball. In addition to his scoring ability, Kemp is also a force on defense.

scored 11 points and had 6 rebounds as he spent thirty-one minutes on the floor.

Kemp's season totals were not spectacular, but they were steady. He had 6.5 points per game while playing an average of fourteen minutes per game (a regulation NBA game is forty-eight minutes long).

Kemp said that the biggest kicks he got during his first year in the NBA came when he slammed home a dunk while being guarded by some of the league's top players. "If that doesn't put a smile on your face, dunking on someone you grew up watching on television, I don't know what does."[5]

Chapter 4

Moving Up

Shawn Kemp had played in 81 games during his rookie season. He was backup to the starter in all but one of them. Seattle had a new coach in 1990–1991—K. C. Jones, a great player for the Boston Celtics in the 1950s and 1960s. Jones also used Kemp as a substitute rather than a starter as the season opened.

Fifteen games into the season, however, the situation changed. The SuperSonics traded Xavier McDaniel to the Phoenix Suns, opening a spot in the team's front line. Derrick McKey moved from power forward to small forward, his more natural position. This enabled Kemp to move into the starting lineup as the team's top power forward.

Kemp responded quickly to the opportunity. He

wanted to show Coach Jones and his teammates that he could perform well as a starter. In his first game as a starter, Kemp played well. The SuperSonics lost but Kemp scored 18 points and grabbed 8 rebounds in the thirty-eight minutes that he played.

He did even better in the next game, finishing with 31 points and 10 rebounds in a win over the Milwaukee Bucks. In his first two games in the starting lineup, Kemp totaled 49 points and 18 rebounds. He kept up the good work in the following weeks. He was averaging nearly 20 points and over 10 rebounds per game.

Although he did not maintain that pace over the rest of the season, Kemp did improve his statistics in all categories. He more than doubled his playing time to over thirty minutes per game and his scoring average to 15 points per game. His shooting accuracy increased as well. Kemp made more than 50 percent of his field goal attempts. In addition, he led the SuperSonics with 679 rebounds, an average of 8.4 per game.

Kemp also provided a strong defensive presence by blocking opponents' shots. In a game on January 18 against the Los Angeles Lakers, Kemp set a SuperSonic record by blocking 10 shots.

His dunks were still the most spectacular part of his game, however. In February he made his

Leaping high into the air, Shawn Kemp shoots over the opposition.

second-straight appearance in the NBA Slam Dunk Championships. He put on a dazzling display and came in second to Dee Brown of the Boston Celtics.

From the start of the season, though, he made it clear that he had more than slam dunks on his mind. Kemp said:

> The dunk is fun, but this year I don't think I'll be dunking as much, because I'm going to be playing more minutes and I've got to save some energy. Dunking's just part of the game. If I get an opportunity to do it, I'll do it. I mean, when you've been dunking as long as I have, maybe it looks fancier than it really is. But now I want people to see that I can play every phase of the game, not just the dunk.[1]

Seattle wrapped up the regular season with nine wins in its final thirteen games. The strong finish earned the SuperSonics a spot in the playoffs.

In the first round, the SuperSonics went up against the Portland Trail Blazers in a best-of-five series. Portland won the first two games, but Seattle—back on its home court—won the next two to tie up the series. In the final game in Portland, the Trail Blazers came out on top, 119–107, finally ending the SuperSonics' season.

Kemp averaged 13.4 points and 7.2 rebounds per game in the playoff series. Those were totals that

FACT

In addition to being a fan favorite, Shawn Kemp is popular with producers of basketball highlight films. Kemp is often one of the first players they will look to in putting together any highlights showing spectacular dunk shots.

After the 1990–1991 season, Shawn Kemp and the Seattle SuperSonics faced the Portland Trail Blazers in the first round of the playoffs. Despite a strong effort by the Sonics, Portland won the series in five games.

many players would envy, but they were below what Kemp had averaged during the regular season. One of the reasons was that Kemp had some powerful competition.

Against the Trail Blazers, Kemp was up against one of the toughest power forwards in the league—Buck Williams. It was the youth and energy of Kemp against the experience and strength of Williams. Both had great respect for the other.

"I couldn't allow him to have the freedom under the basket," Williams said of Kemp. "I had to maintain some kind of contact with him around the basket, because with his leaping ability, I'm in trouble."[2] Likewise, Kemp had high praise for his opponent.

> When you play against somebody like Buck Williams, you automatically are going to have a tough time. He's strong and he works hard. I look forward to playing against guys who love to run up and down the court and bang—and keep it clean. Buck's that way. . . . I think I held my ground very well, for being my second year. I wouldn't . . . say he outplayed me or I outplayed him. It was pretty much just a battle.[3]

Chapter 5

More Hard Work

Coach Jones was happy with the way Kemp held his own against Williams. He also knew that Kemp still had more work to do. Over the summer of 1991, Jones asked an old friend to come to Seattle and work out with Kemp. Dave Cowens, a Hall of Fame center who had played many years for the Celtics, spent three days with Kemp, helping him with his inside game.

It was not just the hard driving contact near the basket that Kemp tried to improve. He also worked on perfecting a jump shot from farther out. Kemp usually encountered heavy traffic when trying to dunk. Having a good outside shot would help open the middle and make him even more effective. He played in summer leagues in Utah and Los Angeles, and developed into a more complete player by the time he went to training camp with the SuperSonics in the fall 1991.

"I'm still trying to get more comfortable making decisions on the court," Kemp said.[1] The difference was apparent during the exhibition season. He led Seattle in scoring, field-goal percentage, rebounding, and shotblocking in the team's preseason games.

One of those games was against Portland on October 20. Kemp scored 18 points, including the game-winning basket on an alley-oop play in an 89–87 win. Kemp and the SuperSonics could not wait for the regular season to begin. Then, in the team's final exhibition game, disaster struck.

Kemp was thrilling the fans in a small arena in Spokane, Washington, with a series of sensational dunks. After one of them he landed on a slick spot of the court and collapsed onto the floor. The Sonics first feared that he had broken his foot. Kemp was just as scared as the team flew back to Seattle after the game.

Kemp relaxed the next day when X rays showed that the foot was not broken. However, he still had a severe sprain and had to sit out the first twelve games of the regular season.

Kemp returned to the lineup on November 26, on

Moving with the ball, Shawn Kemp looks for the open man. In the summer of 1991 Kemp worked on his outside shooting in order to make him a more dangerous offensive player.

his twenty-second birthday. Kemp was happy to be back and was also happy that the game was against the Golden State Warriors. One of the Warriors' rookies was Billy Owens, a longtime friend of Kemp's. The pair had played with and against each other in national tournaments, starting when they were in eighth grade. Owens, who signed with the Warriors after his junior year of college, was the first of Kemp's peers to join him in the NBA. "Finally," said Kemp, "I got to play against someone my own age."[2]

Kemp got the most out of his return to the court. Even though he played only twenty-three minutes, he scored 21 points and stole the ball from Billy Owens four times. His biggest play came near the end of the third quarter. With Seattle trailing by three points, Kemp stole the ball from Owens. He broke down court and slammed the ball through the basket for his seventh dunk of the game. The SuperSonics went on to win the game in overtime, 136–130.

"He was way beyond what I had expected," Coach Jones said of Kemp's performance. "He just came in flying. He was just spectacular out there. That was just the tonic we needed."[3]

Jones added:

> He learns, and learns fast, from his mistakes. I don't want to see Shawn get wrapped up in the spectacular because that takes away from the

basics: learning how to box out, learning how to play defense. When you have the gliding power that Shawn has, you have to understand the little things. When you get the base firmly in place, then—if you have talent, which Shawn does—you become a great player.[4]

Kemp agreed with his coach's assessment. "I don't have a lot of things down yet. It's just a matter of time. It's coming. I just have to keep working hard."[5] Kemp did keep working hard, and the results were showing. He quickly returned to his preseason form but then encountered more problems.

The SuperSonics were playing the New York Knicks at Madison Square Garden in New York City. Kemp was matched up against his former teammate Xavier McDaniel, who had been traded yet again, to the Knicks. With barely over three minutes to play and only one point separating the two teams, McDaniel and Kemp battled under the New York basket. As McDaniel faked a shot, Kemp jumped in an attempt to block it.

He took a swipe, but there was no shot to block. Instead Kemp's hand crashed into the metal rim of the basket. The impact sliced the skin between the last two fingers on his right hand. It was a serious gash that caused Kemp to miss the next six games.

FACT

Seattle fans came up with a nickname for Kemp that played on the large amounts of rain that fall in this city. Instead of "Rain Man," Kemp became known as "Reign Man." He was the man who reigned over basketball in the Great Northwest.

What had started off as such a promising year was turning into a nightmare season for him. Kemp returned to the lineup in late December and had no more injury problems the rest of the season. By that time, however, his conditioning and his confidence were affected.

Being without Kemp over much of the first part of the season hurt the SuperSonics. When a team struggles, it is often the coach who gets the blame. K. C. Jones was reminded of that when he was replaced in January 1992 by George Karl. Soon after, Karl added Tim Grgurich—who had once tried to recruit Kemp for the University of Nevada-Las Vegas—to the coaching staff as an assistant.

Kemp played better under the new coaches. In a game on January 31 against the Charlotte Hornets, he had 22 points and 21 rebounds. It was the first game of his career in which he went over over twenty points and rebounds for a double-double.

Kemp really turned on the steam over the final month of the season. In Seattle's final eighteen games, as the team battled to return to the playoffs, Kemp averaged 18.3 points and 12.9 rebounds per game. One of those games was a 14-point, 12-rebound performance against the Los Angeles Lakers as Seattle won its eleventh game out of its last fifteen.

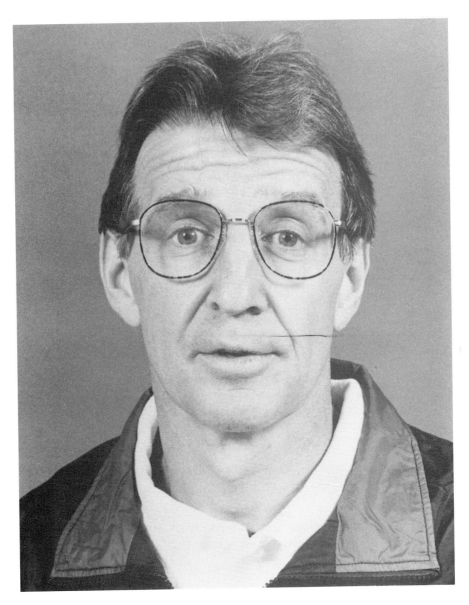

When George Karl became head coach in 1992 he brought in Tim Grgurich (shown here) to be one of his assistants. Kemp improved his game under the new coaching staff.

After the game, some people even suggested that Kemp had had an off game since he had been playing even better than that. Karl laughed when he heard those comments. "If a bad game for Shawn Kemp is 14 points and 12 rebounds," he said, "then we're on our way. In other words, when people start comparing you to yourself, you're starting to get somewhere."[6]

Kemp was playing outstanding basketball even though he had a throat infection that was zapping some of his strength. He was not eating as much as he usually did. This, combined with the grind of a hard season, caused him to lose nearly thirty pounds in a five-week period.

Still he had a strong finish to the season. Although he had played in only 64 games during the year, he was the SuperSonics' leading rebounder in 39 of them. He also finished fourteenth in the National Basketball Association in average number of blocked shots per game.

He had 28 points and 16 rebounds in the final regular-season game, against the Golden State Warriors. As it turned out, he was just warming up for an even greater performance against Golden State.

The Warriors were Seattle's opening-round playoff opponent. The SuperSonics were considered underdogs to Golden State, which had tied with Utah for the second-best record in the Western Conference. Opening the series on the road, the SuperSonics surprised the Warriors with a 117–109 win. Kemp, with 28 points and 16 rebounds, was outstanding.

He was even better on the boards, pulling down 19 rebounds in the second game. However, Golden State won this one to tie the series.

The third game, at the Seattle Center Coliseum, was a close one. Kemp's friend Billy Owens put the Warriors ahead by one point in the final seconds. After Seattle inbounded the ball, however, Kemp drove to the basket and drew a foul. He stepped to the line and calmly sank both shots to give Seattle a 129–128 win.

The Sonics needed just one more victory to finish off the Warriors. They got it, thanks to Kemp. He was magnificent, scoring 21 points and collecting 20 rebounds. The SuperSonics had upset Golden State, winning the series, three games to one.

In the conference semifinals, a best-of-seven series, they would face another powerful team—the Utah Jazz. In the playoffs the year before Kemp had had his hands full with Buck Williams. Now he would be matched against the best power forward in the game—Karl Malone. This time he had more trouble. Malone outmuscled Kemp under the boards as Utah finished off Seattle in six games.

Karl Malone of the Utah Jazz fights for position against Kevin Garnett of the Minnesota Timberwolves. Malone is considered to be one of the best power forwards to ever play basketball.

Although he was not yet in Malone's class as a power forward, Kemp drew praise for his gutsy play throughout a very challenging season. Team officials were also optimistic about the future with Kemp leading the Sonics.

Team president Bob Whitsitt echoed the thoughts of others in basketball when he said, "There's no reason Shawn can't take his game to the level where he wants to take it."[7]

Chapter 6

Establishing a Reputation

After his encounter with Karl Malone in the playoffs, Kemp was determined to add to his strength before the 1992–1993 season. He worked with Seattle's strength and conditioning coach Bob Medina in an intensive weight-training program. Kemp not only regained the weight he had lost near the end of the previous season, he added ten more pounds. Now he would be ready for the biggest and best the NBA had to offer, including Karl Malone.

Over the summer he also spent a great deal of time on the practice court with assistant coach Tim Grgurich. Kemp and Grgurich got along well. Grgurich noted that he was not the only one who hit it off with Kemp. "One of the things that makes him special is how much everyone on the team wants him to succeed," Grgurich said. "I think the older players have been a real help to Shawn Kemp. They sense how good he can be, and they've helped him along."[1]

As he started his fourth season in the league, Kemp knew his efforts to improve were paying off.

> When I first came into the NBA, no one gave me much credit. Everybody told me it was going to be four or five years before I was going to be able to play. I felt I had to take things into my own hands. I knew that, being young, it was going to take a lot of hard work. Of course, back then, I didn't know how hard.[2]

Kemp put on a great show in the season opener against the Houston Rockets in Yokohama, Japan, and continued to keep up the strong pace.

George Karl noted how Kemp had thrilled the Japanese fans as well as what he was doing to help the team. "He plays with a tremendous flair and entertainment factor that I love," Karl said. "But what I like better is that Shawn is solid, mentally, on the game. Winning is the reason he plays."[3]

Winning was what Kemp was helping the SuperSonics to do. The team got off to a fast start. Instead of just contending for one of the eight

FACT

Shawn Kemp has shown consistent improvement in his career. He was starting his fourth season in 1992-1993, and had raised his rebounding and scoring average since entering the NBA. He would continue to do this through his first seven years in the league.

playoff spots in the Western Conference, Seattle had its sights set on finishing first in the Pacific Division.

The team's chief rival in the division was the Phoenix Suns, led by Charles Barkley. While some experts did not see how anyone in the conference could beat the Suns, the SuperSonics were staying close to them in the standings.

The success was a team effort. The Sonics won consistently, even during a period in December when the team was without two of its biggest players. Centers Michael Cage and Benoit Benjamin both had leg ailments. Kemp also missed a few games with a hyperextended right knee.

By the end of December the SuperSonics had a record of 18 wins and 8 losses and trailed the Phoenix Suns by three-and-a-half games.

On January 20 the SuperSonics beat the Lakers, 111–101, in Los Angeles. Kemp scored 24 points, ten of them on thundering slam dunks. Two of them were of the alley-oop variety; two more came after Kemp rebounded a missed shot and stuffed the ball back through the hoop in a manner that made the backboard shake.

His greatest acrobatic feat was not a dunk, though. Late in the game, he chased down a missed Laker shot as it was bouncing out of bounds. Kemp grabbed the ball, but there was no way he could

Concentrating only on the basket, Shawn Kemp looks to sink a foul shot. Kemp seemed like a much more focused player coming into the 1992–1993 season. His focus was on winning.

stop. If he went out of bounds, the ball would be turned back to Los Angeles.

Instead, Kemp jumped into the air and threw the ball backward onto the court *between his legs*. Teammate Gary Payton grabbed the incredible pass, took it down court, and sank an eighteen-foot jump shot. The play sealed a win that drew the SuperSonics to within a half-game of the Suns in the Pacific Division standings.

While fans marveled at Kemp's great pass, Payton took it in stride. "That's Shawn," he said after the game. "I called for it, and he delivered the ball. He's just one of those exciting players."[4]

Kemp was invited to once again participate in the NBA Slam Dunk Championship on All-Star Weekend at the Delta Center in Salt Lake City, Utah. This year, though, he stayed around for more than just the dunking contest. Kemp had earned a spot on the Western Conference All-Star team. He was the SuperSonics' first All-Star since Dale Ellis in 1989. Kemp played nine minutes in the All-Star Game and pulled down 2 rebounds.

The SuperSonics were making a strong run at first place during this time. A week before the All-Star break, they trailed Phoenix by seven games as they prepared to face the Suns at the Seattle Center Coliseum. Phoenix was hot, having won its last five

Drafted by Seattle in 1990, Gary Payton has evolved into one the NBA's premier point guards. He and Kemp have teamed up on many exciting plays.

games. The Sonics, on the other hand, were hoping to halt a two-game losing streak. Kemp had a fine game with 23 points and 14 rebounds.

Yet it was others who decided the game at the end. Charles Barkley put the Suns ahead by a point with a seventeen-foot jump shot with five seconds left in the game. The Sonics did not quit, though. With less than a half-second on the clock, Derrick McKey drove and sank a layup to give Seattle a 95–94 win.

The victory provided the SuperSonics with a real boost. It was the beginning of a ten-game winning streak that pulled them back to within three-and-a-half games of the Suns. The final win in the streak was a 149–93 trouncing of the Philadelphia 76ers. The 56-point margin of victory tied a SuperSonic record.

Despite the hot run, Seattle still finished seven games behind Phoenix in the Pacific Division when the regular season ended. They were in the playoffs, though, and Kemp had had another fine season. For the third straight year he improved in nearly every category. Besides being second on the Sonics in scoring, he was twelfth in the NBA in both rebounding and blocked shots.

The Sonics' first-round playoff opponent would be the Utah Jazz, the team that had eliminated them from the playoffs the year before. Once again it would be Shawn Kemp versus Karl Malone in a battle under the boards.

Kemp and the SuperSonics won the first matchup. Kemp had an outstanding game, scoring 29 points and adding 17 rebounds. He made all 9 of his free-throw attempts and also blocked 3 Utah shots as Seattle won, 99–85.

Utah took the next two games and was only one win away from knocking out the Sonics. Seattle played tough, winning the fourth game on the road to stay alive. Back in Seattle for the final game, the SuperSonics got off to a slow start. They scored only thirty points in the first half and trailed by nine. In the second half, though, they stormed back with seventy points and won the game, 100–92.

The rest of the playoffs would be best-of-seven series. For their next round, against the Houston Rockets, the Sonics had the overall home-court advantage. It turned out to be important as the home team won every game in the series.

The series was even at three games apiece with the seventh game at the Seattle Center Coliseum. Houston led in the game through most of the first half, but a Sonic surge put them in front by the end of the third quarter. Houston came back in the fourth period, and the game was tied at the end of regulation time.

Each team scored a basket in overtime before Ricky Pierce sank a pair of free throws to put Seattle ahead by two points. Kemp then connected on a twelve-foot jumper over Hakeem Olajuwon, the Rocket center, to open up a four-point margin. Houston was not able to catch up again, although the team did come close.

Seattle clung to a 101–100 lead when Derrick McKey stepped to the free-throw line with fourteen seconds left. McKey missed both shots, and the Rockets had another chance. Vernon Maxwell took a shot that could have put Houston ahead. The shot clanged off the rim, though, and disappeared into Kemp's arms. Kemp was fouled with less than one second left and he buried both free throws. The SuperSonics had a 103–100 overtime win and a victory in the playoff series.

For the third year in a row, the SuperSonics were advancing deeper into the playoffs. Now they would face the mighty Suns in the conference championship round with a trip to the NBA Finals on the line.

This series seesawed back and forth. The Suns won the first game. The second game went down to the wire, and the Sonics emerged victorious. Kemp made six pressure free throws down the stretch, including a pair that gave Seattle a 97–96 lead with less than two minutes to play. Phoenix retook the lead, but Sam Perkins of the SuperSonics drilled a three-point shot with 9.8 seconds left. Phoenix tried to tie it, but Danny Ainge missed a shot. Kemp was fouled in the battle for the rebound and sank both shots to wrap up a 103–99 win for the SuperSonics.

The teams again alternated victories in the third and fourth games. Phoenix was in control of the fifth game, but Kemp did what he could to put Seattle back in it. He scored twenty points in the final quarter, including a basket that pulled the SuperSonics to within one point with 34 seconds left. Then Dan Majerle countered with a three-point basket, his eighth of the game, to seal it up for Phoenix.

Facing elimination, Kemp and the SuperSonics stepped up in the sixth game. Kemp had 22 points and 15 rebounds, as Seattle won, 118–102. For the third straight series, the Sonics were going to the limit. Kemp looked forward to the challenge.

> If you can't get up for the seventh game, you can't get up at all. There isn't any pressure at this point. Everyone wants to make it. It's just who wants to win more.[5]

Charles Barkley of the Suns showed how badly he wanted to win. This time he had only one assist,

Gliding through the lane, Shawn Kemp splits the defense on his way to an easy basket.

preferring to keep the ball and do things himself. Barkley scored 44 points and had 24 rebounds to lead Phoenix to a win in the game and a spot in the NBA Finals.

The SuperSonics were disappointed, but proud of the team's efforts. Kemp proved that he could play under pressure, and the other teams in the league knew that they would be hearing from this team again.

Chapter 7

Sonic Setbacks

The SuperSonics stayed hot as the 1993–1994 season opened. Despite the fact that Kemp missed a few games in December with a bruised knee, Seattle won thirty of its first thirty-five games.

Kemp had fully recovered from the knee injury by the All-Star break in February. He continued his strong play through the remainder of the regular season. Another injury could not even slow him down.

An inflamed elbow kept him on the bench at the start of a game against Sacramento in early March. He entered the game midway through the first period with Seattle behind. Kemp scored his team's final seven points of the quarter to allow the SuperSonics to tie the game. Seattle fell behind again in the second quarter and trailed by four points at halftime.

Kemp forgot about the pain in his elbow and came alive. He scored 14 points and had 9 rebounds in the third quarter alone. He played less than a minute of the fourth quarter. His third-quarter surge, though, had given his team an eleven-point lead. The Sonics were able to hang on the rest of the way without him.

Two weeks later, Kemp achieved the first triple-double of his career. He had racked up many double-doubles in his career. Yet in this game against Charlotte, he had double figures in three categories—15 points, 11 rebounds, and 12 assists.

Kemp followed that up soon after with a four-game stretch in which he averaged 27 points and over 12 rebounds. For his efforts he was named NBA Player of the Week.

Kemp finished the season as Seattle's leading scorer and rebounder. He was also among the league leaders in scoring, rebounding, and field-goal percentage. The Sonics had a win-loss record of 63–19, the best in the team's history. The record was also the best regular-season one in the NBA, putting Seattle in a prime position as the playoffs opened.

The SuperSonics won the first two games of their

FACT

All-Star Weekend was a busy one for Kemp in 1994. On Saturday he competed in the Slam Dunk Championship. He finished second to Isaiah (J.R.) Rider, of the Minnesota Timberwolves. The next day he started in the All-Star Game for the first time ever. He grabbed 12 rebounds in just twenty-two minutes of play.

best-of-five series against the Denver Nuggets in the opening playoff round. Then the Nuggets came back to win three in a row—the last two in overtime. The abrupt end was a crushing way for the SuperSonics to finish the year.

Kemp did have other activities that summer to take his mind off the disappointing finish. He was a member of the United States team that would compete in the 1994 World Championship of Basketball in Toronto. The United States squad that played in the Olympics two years before was known as the Dream Team. The 1994 squad became known as Dream Team II.

United States' coach Don Nelson liked Kemp's style and made him the team's starting center, ahead of Shaquille O'Neal of the Orlando Magic. Kemp was also named to the All-Tournament team as the United States easily won the championship.

During this time, Kemp almost became a member of a new NBA team. In late June it was reported that Kemp had been traded by Seattle to the Chicago Bulls for Scottie Pippen. Kemp heard the news after a Dream Team II practice. As it turned out the SuperSonics backed out of the deal at the last minute.

Kemp remained with Seattle, but was hurt by the fact that the team almost got rid of him. The

FACT

Kemp was a key member of Dream Team II, coached by Don Nelson of the Golden State Warriors, in 1994. Other members of the team were:

Derrick Coleman—New Jersey Nets
Joe Dumars—Detroit Pistons
Kevin Johnson—Phoenix Suns
Larry Johnson—Charlotte Hornets
Dan Majerle—Phoenix Suns
Reggie Miller—Indiana Pacers
Alonzo Mourning—Charlotte Hornets
Shaquille O'Neal—Orlando Magic
Mark Price—Cleveland Cavaliers
Steve Smith—Miami Heat
Dominique Wilkins—Los Angeles Clippers

bitterness lingered over the next few months. By the time the 1994–1995 season opened, though, Kemp was ready to concentrate on basketball again.

In a double-overtime win over the Los Angeles Clippers in December, Kemp had a career-high 42 points. He had eight of those points in the second overtime period. If not for a mistake on his part in the first overtime, though, Seattle might have won the game then. He followed a monster dunk by taunting a Clipper player and received a technical foul. This allowed the Clippers to score an extra point that helped them send the game into a second overtime period.

At the same time that Kemp was emerging as a top star in the NBA, his taunting reminded fans of how young he still was. The SuperSonics hoped that he would mature and drop this type of behavior as he got older.

Seattle played great ball again with the team revolving around three stars: Kemp, forward Detlef Schrempf, and guard Gary Payton.

All three played in the All-Star Game in February, with Kemp scoring 13 points in the game.

Kemp really picked up his game down the stretch. He came alive at a time the SuperSonics needed a lift. They had been sluggish for the past month as they went to New York for a game on March 11. It did not look like they would be snapping out of their funk in the early going. Kemp missed all five shots that he took in the first quarter. In the second quarter, though, he found his touch. He had nine points in the first 4.5 minutes of play. Kemp finished the game with 22 points and 19 rebounds to lead Seattle to a 96–84 victory.

The next night the Sonics were in Detroit. Many of Kemp's family and friends had come up from Elkhart to watch him. He made sure that they were

In November 1993 the Sonics acquired Detlef Schrempf. Schrempf won the NBA's sixth man award, given to the league's top reserve, in both 1990 and 1991.

not disappointed. Kemp put on quite a show in the third quarter. He had six slam dunks, which silenced most of the Detroit crowd, but thrilled his personal cheering section. Kemp finished the game with 25 points and 16 rebounds as the SuperSonics won by forty points.

Kemp and the SuperSonics were back on the right track. The New York game was the first of nine-straight games in which Kemp had at least 10 points and 10 rebounds.

"This is the time of year when a lot of players start getting tired," said Kemp. "I like this time of year. This is when I like to take over."[1] Kemp was taking over. He had double-doubles in sixteen of eighteen games, with the SuperSonics winning fifteen of those games.

Kemp finished the regular season with a scoring average of 18.7 points per game. It was the fifth-straight year that he had improved his scoring. His rebounding average also went up for the fifth year in a row. He finished sixth in the NBA with 10.9 rebounds per game. The SuperSonics won 57 games in the regular season and were in good shape entering the playoffs.

Against the Los Angeles Lakers, Kemp scored 21 points as Seattle won the first game easily. Kemp continued to play well, but the road got rougher for

From his rookie year until 1996 Shawn Kemp improved his scoring and rebounding averages each year.

the rest of the SuperSonics. The Lakers won the next three games to capture the playoff series.

Kemp averaged 24.8 points and 12 rebounds in the four games. Despite that, the SuperSonic season had a disappointing finish. Seattle fans were expecting more of the SuperSonics.

Chapter 8

A Title Run

In 1995 Kemp went back to Indiana during the off-season. He did not spend too much time relaxing, though. Kemp ran five miles every day, even during a record heat wave in the Midwest.

"My mom was always telling me I was crazy, but you just get mad if you sit around the house and think."[1] Kemp was also driven by the memory of the SuperSonics' playoff loss to the Lakers. Like the rest of his teammates, he was still stinging from two-straight seasons of an early exit from the playoffs.

Kemp was determined things would be different the next season. He was willing to work hard to make himself an even better player. "You never want to be satisfied with yourself," he said. "I'm still young enough to improve, and I know that I can. It's

FACT

Kemp's boyhood idol was Julius Erving ("Dr. J") of the Philadelphia 76ers. Erving went to see a SuperSonics' game in Philadelphia in 1995. Kemp put on quite a show for his boyhood hero. In addition to 29 points and 12 rebounds, he blocked 5 shots and had 3 steals. Erving was so impressed that he visited the Seattle locker room after the game.

just a fact of doing it in the off-season and carrying it out in the regular season."[2]

Besides running, Kemp spent a lot of time working out and lost nearly thirty pounds over the summer. Three years before, he had spent the off-season putting on weight so that he could match muscle with the strongest power forwards in the league. Now he was slimming down, swapping bulk for speed and endurance.

With help from his sister Lisa, he also worked on his free-throw shooting. Kemp would wait for her to come home each evening. Then the two would go to the playground at Pinewood Elementary School. Kemp would shoot from the foul line, and Lisa would toss the ball back to him. "It would be 100 degrees outside, but we were out there every night," he said.[3]

With the free-throw shooting out of the way, Shawn and Lisa would then square off in a one-on-one game. "She pushes me," Kemp said of his sister. "She taught me how to play ball. I've got a lot of support from my entire family. Both my sister and my mom have taught me a lot."[4]

The summer of support and hard work paid off. Kemp and the SuperSonics were ready for a new season. They would also be playing in a newly renovated arena. The SuperSonics had played the 1994–1995 season in the Tacoma Dome while the

Going into the 1995–1996 season, Shawn Kemp felt that he needed to work on his free throw shooting. During the off-season he kept in shape by practicing his foul shooting with his sister Lisa. Kemp credits Lisa with teaching him to play basketball.

Seattle Center Coliseum was torn apart for major remodeling. In 1995 they moved back into the building, which was now known as KeyArena. They were back in the shadow of Seattle's great landmark—the Space Needle—and feeling right at home.

A sellout crowd was on hand for Seattle's first game in KeyArena. The SuperSonics responded by beating the Lakers, the team that had ended their previous season. Kemp was outstanding, scoring 23 points and grabbing 13 rebounds.

The Seattle leaders were again Kemp, Payton, and Schrempf. Each proved able to pick up his game when something happened to one of the others. For example, the night before Thanksgiving, Payton left a game in Minnesota in the third quarter. It was first feared he had broken his foot; it turned out to be only a sprain, but Payton was done for the evening.

With Payton gone, Kemp took charge. The game was tied with four minutes left. Kemp reeled off the next nine points with three clutch baskets and three free throws. He finished the game with 26 points, as Seattle won, 106–97.

Three days later, on Kemp's twenty-sixth birthday, the SuperSonics played the Chicago Bulls. The Bulls came into the game with a win-loss record of 10–1 and held a thirteen-point lead at halftime. The Sonics stormed back in the second half, though, and won the game, 97–92. Kemp made 10 of 13 field goal attempts, and finished the game with 25 points and 14 rebounds.

After the game the Seattle players had a party at which they celebrated both the comeback victory and Kemp's birthday. Kemp ended up with another reason to celebrate: he was named NBA Player of the Week. In four games during the week Kemp averaged over 23 points and nearly 13 rebounds. He was red hot in his shooting, sinking more than 60 percent of his shots from the field. He was leading the league in rebounding and among the league leaders in scoring and field-goal percentage.

The SuperSonics suffered a real blow in December when Detlef Schrempf broke his leg while setting a screen in a game against Portland. Once again Kemp had to step up. In Seattle's next game Kemp had 22 rebounds—a career-high for him. Even so, the SuperSonics lost the game in overtime.

The next night Seattle won, beating the San Antonio Spurs, 88–83. Kemp had 30 points, more than a third of the points scored by the SuperSonics. He also had 3 blocked shots and 16 rebounds, prompting coach George Karl to observe that Kemp was playing as well as anyone in the NBA.[5]

Kemp got more praise from his coach after the Sonics' next game against the Golden State Warriors.

The home of the Seattle SuperSonics, the KeyArena, is shown here.

The Warriors were determined to stop Kemp. They double-teamed Kemp and sometimes sent three defenders after him when he got the ball. Kemp responded by passing the ball out to Payton or Sam Perkins, who were left open because of all the attention Kemp was receiving.

Golden State's strategy was still paying off, however. The Warriors held a five-point lead at halftime. As the third quarter opened, though, there was no stopping Kemp. He connected on a fadeaway basket from four feet out, delivered a pass to Perkins for a dunk, slammed home a dunk shot himself, and then bounced a nice pass out of a double-team that resulted in an easy layup for Perkins. Later in the game, Kemp kicked out to Perkins and Payton, who each took Kemp's pass and sank a three-point basket.

Even with more than one player hanging on him most of the game, Kemp still scored 32 points. He also had 7 assists as he contributed to his teammates' scoring. "That was the best game I have ever seen Shawn Kemp play," said Karl. "It was the complete package."[6]

Fans were noticing not only how well Kemp was playing, but how much he was maturing. In the past he had received technical fouls for taunting opposing players, but no longer. He was learning to keep

Sharp shooter Sam Perkins is one of the key members of the Seattle SuperSonics. Perkins is one of Seattle's best three-point shooters.

his comments to himself and let his great play speak for him.

Kemp continued to be triple-teamed, but he knew how to handle it. "I'm seeing triple-teams this year," he said. "That's a first. I know if I kick the ball out, re-establish position in the post, then get the ball back, it could be as easy as making a head fake, then going up for a dunk."[7]

In February Kemp started in the All-Star Game for the third straight year. Things were going well for Kemp and the SuperSonics, who had the best record in the Western Conference. "We're playing with a bit more confidence, and we're more loose," Kemp said of his team's performance. "Teams buckle down in the second half, so it's going to be harder. Everyone's trying to get into the playoffs and make a run. No doubt it's going to be tougher, but we're looking forward to it."[8]

The team that really buckled down was Seattle. They were in the midst of a winning streak that lasted over a month. For the second time during the season, Kemp was named Player of the Week during the hot streak. However, the string of victories was a team effort. This time it was others who had to step up when Kemp went down with an injury.

In a game on March 1 in Boston, Kemp got off to a great start. He had nine points and seven rebounds in the first quarter. However, after completing a fast break with a resounding dunk near the end of the first quarter, Kemp landed awkwardly and sprained his left foot. The SuperSonics still went on to win the game. It was their twelfth-straight victory, which tied a team record. The next night they broke the record with their thirteenth win in a row. Kemp did not play as the SuperSonics beat the New Jersey Nets.

The winning streak reached fourteen games with a 107–101 overtime win against the Cleveland Cavaliers. Kemp came back to play 21 minutes in the game. He scored 9 points and had 6 rebounds, even though his foot was still bothering him. George Karl was named Coach of the Month for February, but he had other things on his mind. He was concerned about Kemp reinjuring his foot and kept him out of the next two games.

With Kemp gone again the winning streak finally ended. Washington beat Seattle and stopped the string at fourteen-straight wins. The SuperSonics still had a commanding lead in the Pacific Division, however. They were nine-and-a-half games ahead of the Los Angeles Lakers.

However, their margin was not as big over the top teams in the Midwest Division, the San Antonio Spurs and Utah Jazz. The Sonics were determined to finish with a better record than the Spurs and Jazz.

FACT

Shawn Kemp won the NBA Player of the Week Award twice during the 1995–1996 season. The first time was for the week ending November 26. Kemp averaged 23.3 points and 12.8 rebounds in four games that week. He later averaged 22.5 points and 13 rebounds per game and won the award for the week ending February 25.

If they could do so, they would have the home-court advantage throughout the Western Conference play-off series.

Winning would not be easy, though. The Spurs were playing especially well. While Seattle had won all of its games in February, San Antonio went on a seventeen-game winning streak that covered the entire month of March.

Still, the Spurs could not come up with a better record than the SuperSonics. Seattle, although it suffered a few losses, produced a few big wins during this time.

They trailed the Orlando Magic, 99–92, late in a game on March 13. Seattle then scored the final eight points of the game to win, 100–99. A few days later the Los Angeles Clippers had the Sonics on the ropes. This time Seattle scored the final seven points of the game to win, 104–101. Kemp scored five of those last seven points in a span of just twenty-eight seconds.

Seattle had back-to-back games against the Utah Jazz in late March and early April. The SuperSonics won the first one by two points as Sam Perkins connected on a three-point basket with 12 seconds left in the game. The next one was easier as Seattle cruised to a 100–81 win.

Even after their fourteen-game winning streak had been snapped in early March, the SuperSonics remained on fire. They won eighteen of their last twenty-three games to finish the regular season with 64 wins—a team record.

For Kemp, it was an outstanding individual season. He finished fifth in the league with 11.4 rebounds per game, and fifth with a .561 field-goal percentage. He also averaged 19.6 points a game—his highest scoring total ever.

Kemp hoped the off-season would not come too quickly as the regular season ended. For the last two seasons the SuperSonics had been knocked out in the opening round of the playoffs. They wanted to stay around longer in 1996.

Right off the bat, though, they would be at a disadvantage. Kemp would not be in the lineup for Seattle's first playoff game. In the final game of the regular season, Kemp had gotten into a scuffle with Tom Hammonds of the Denver Nuggets. As a result, he was suspended for one game.

Even without Kemp, Seattle won the playoff opener over the Sacramento Kings. The Sonics ended up beating the Kings, three games to one, to win the series and advance in the playoffs.

The Sonics' opponent in the conference semifinals would be the Houston Rockets. The Rockets had won the NBA championship for the last two years. However, they were no match for the

SuperSonics. Seattle swept the Rockets in four games. The final game came on George Karl's forty-fifth birthday. It was a nice present for the coach, but it was not without some scary moments. Seattle blew a twenty-point lead in the second half, and the game went into overtime.

The SuperSonics clung to a one-point lead with just over a minute to play in the overtime period when Kemp gave them some breathing room. He made a basket, was fouled, and sank a free throw for a four-point Seattle lead. Houston pulled within striking distance again, but Kemp put the game out of reach by sinking two free throws with 13 seconds to play.

Seattle won the game, and the series, to advance to the Western Conference Finals against the Utah Jazz. Once again it would be Shawn Kemp against Karl Malone.

Kemp got off to a fast start in the first game of the series. He made all nine of his field-goal attempts in the first half. Kemp finished the game with 21 points as Seattle beat the Jazz by thirty points.

The second game was closer, and once again Kemp stood out. He broke an 85–85 tie with a turn-around jump shot in the lane with just 1:11 left in the game. Kemp added another basket and a key steal as Seattle came out on top, 91–87.

Utah won the next game, but the SuperSonics

won the fourth game and were on the verge of putting the series away. The Jazz would not make it easy though. Utah won two in a row to tie the series at three games apiece.

The seventh game was another close one. Seattle held on for a 90–86 win. Twice in the final 77 seconds, Kemp went to the free-throw line. On each occasion he sank both free throws to give Seattle a cushion. Kemp finished with 26 points and 14 rebounds as Seattle won, 90–86.

For the first time, Kemp would be playing in the NBA Finals. Throughout the conference playoffs he had averaged nearly 20 points and over 10 rebounds per game. Now he would be matching up against one of the top power forwards in the league, Dennis Rodman of the Chicago Bulls. Rodman is one of the greatest rebounders in the history of basketball as well as an excellent defensive player. Kemp would have his hands full.

So would the SuperSonics. They had won 64 games during the regular season. No team had ever won that many without going on to win the NBA title. The problem was that the Chicago Bulls had done even better in the Eastern Conference.

The Bulls set a new NBA record during the 1995–96 season by winning 72 games. In addition to Rodman, the Bulls had a great star in Scottie Pippen.

They also had Michael Jordan—possibly the best basketball player ever. The Bulls were heavy favorites. They had lost only one game in their opening playoff rounds and were on a roll.

The Bulls continued their hot play against Seattle, winning the first game, 107–90. Kemp had a good game, scoring 32 points. However, he suffered a bruised chest bone during the game. For the rest of the playoff series he would play with protective padding on his chest.

Kemp came back with 29 points in the second game. The SuperSonics played better, but they still lost, 92–88. The series shifted to Seattle, with Chicago holding a two-game lead.

The Bulls made it three games to none with a 108–86 win. They were on the verge of a sweep and seemed to have the NBA title locked up. However, Seattle was not ready to play dead yet. The SuperSonics came out strong in the fourth game and rolled to a 107–86 win. Kemp had 25 points with 11 rebounds. "When things go bad, you have to go back to where you started," he explained after the game. "That's the way we played all season, being aggressive and keeping teams on their heels. We were aggressive on every decision."[9]

Kemp and the SuperSonics stayed aggressive in the fifth game. Kemp made four of his first five shots and scored Seattle's first eight points of the game. The score stayed close through most of the game, but Seattle finally pulled away and won, 89–78.

The series moved back to Chicago, and Bulls' fans were worried. Sportscasters were talking about how well Kemp was playing. They were suggesting that he would be named the Most Valuable Player of the series if Seattle ended up winning.

In the end, though, the Bulls proved to be too much. Chicago won the sixth game, 87–75, for the NBA Championship. They had finally finished off the SuperSonics.

It may have been a disappointing finish, but it was a great season for Seattle and Shawn Kemp. The Sonics drew a lot of respect from the Bulls and the basketball world by winning two games when their backs were to the wall.

Following up on a great season is never easy. Seattle did well again in 1996–1997, but ran into some rough spots along the way. The Sonics finished with the best record in the Pacific Division and tied for the second-best record in the Western Conference. Kemp played well during the first half of the season, but slowed during the second half. He felt that he had not paced himself as well as he usually did at the beginning of the season.

Kemp finished the regular season with an average

This basketball court in Elkhart, Indiana, is named in Kemp's honor.

of 18.7 points and 10 rebounds per game. They were good numbers, but for the first time in his professional career, his scoring and rebounding averages went down, rather than up, from the previous year. Fortunately, Kemp improved during the playoffs, when the SuperSonics really needed his great play.

They met a scrappy Phoenix Suns team in the opening round, a best-of-five series. Seattle lost two of the first three games, and faced elimination. However, the Sonics won game four in Phoenix, in overtime, and went on to win game five at home to advance to the next round. In the five games against Phoenix, Kemp averaged 22.2 points and 14.4 rebounds.

Kemp did well in the next round of the playoffs, against the Houston Rockets. Unfortunately, it was not enough. The Rockets won the series in seven games, ending the Seattle season.

As the season came to an end, there was a bit of uncertainty for Kemp. His contract with the Sonics had been an issue during the entire season. Seattle had spent a great deal of money on free-agent players prior to the start of the season—including $33 million to obtain center Jim McIlvane. Other than leading the Sonics in blocked shots, McIlvane had done little else to help the team. Kemp was hoping Seattle would get a big man who could help inside. McIlvane, despite the millions of dollars he

FACT

Kemp is still a hero in his hometown of Elkhart, Indiana. He returns home every summer and spends time with young people in the area. Concord High School contains a display on Kemp. At the Tolson Park Center one of the outdoor courts is even named after Kemp.

received, was not that man. It was also frustrating for Kemp to see other players making so much money, when those players meant so much less than Kemp did to the Soncis' success. The contract situation created a rift between Kemp and the Seattle management. It led some to wonder whether Kemp would return to Seattle for the 1997-1998 season.

One place he did return, at least during the off-season, was his home state. He has built a home on a thirty-acre ranch for his mother. When Kemp comes home for the summer, he stays at the ranch—which is near Bristol, a few miles outside of Elkhart. Barbara Kemp has quit her hospital job and now oversees her son's off-court activities, including the basketball camp that he operates as well as his fan club. "I love to go back home," Kemp says. "I like to hang around with the same friends I grew up with and just be comfortable."[10]

Kemp also gets involved in community activities, both in Elkhart and in Seattle. During the holiday season he has even put on a Santa Claus costume and distributed toys to youngsters at Seattle community centers. (He is known as "Santa Kemp.") "Helping kids, watching them smile, this makes me feel good about myself. I want kids looking up to me," he has said.[11]

Chapter Notes

Chapter 1

1. Mike Kahn, "Super Sonic," *Sport*, March 1992, p. 90.

2. W. Blake Gray, "Kemp, Sonics Fly High in Seattle," *Seattle Times*, November 7, 1992, p. B1.

3. Jack McCallum, "Sonic Boom," *Sports Illustrated*, November 27, 1989, p. 70.

4. Mike Kahn, "The Sky's the Limit," *The Sporting News*, March 15, 1993, p. 35.

5. Ibid.

6. Glenn Nelson, "Straining for Stardom," *Seattle Times*, November 5, 1992, p. E1.

Chapter 2

1. Phillip M. Hoose, *Hoosiers: The Fabulous Basketball Life of Indiana* (New York: Vintage Books, 1986), p. 56.

2. Glenn Nelson, "Straining for Stardom," *Seattle Times*, November 5, 1992, p. E1.

3. Glenn Nelson, "Man Child," *Seattle Times*, March 3, 1991, p. C1.

4. Bill Knight, "Coming of Age," *Seattle Post-Intelligencer*, November 4, 1993, p. D1.

5. Ibid.

6. Tim Keown, "Reign Man," *Sports Illustrated*, February 19, 1996, p. 72.

7. Knight, p. D1.

8. Jack McCallum, "Sonic Boom," *Sports Illustrated*, November 27, 1989, p. 82.

9. Ibid.

10. Ibid., p. 78.

Chapter 3

1. Jack McCallum, "Sonic Boom," *Sports Illustrated*, November 27, 1989, p. 81.

2. Ibid., p. 78.

3. Mike Kahn, "The Sky's the Limit," *The Sporting News*, March 15, 1993, p. 35.

4. John Peoples, "Kemp Earns Spurs, But Sonics Fall," *Seattle Times*, March 16, 1990, p. D1.

5. Glenn Nelson, "Straining for Stardom," *Seattle Times*, November 5, 1992, p. E1.

Chapter 4

1. Steve Kelley, "Sonics' Future Tied to Man-Child Kemp's Maturity," *Seattle Times*, October 31, 1990, p. B1.

2. Art Thiel, "Playing a Grade Higher," *Seattle Post-Intelligencer*, October 21, 1991, p. C2.

3. Ibid.

Chapter 5

1. Art Thiel, "Playing a Grade Higher," *Seattle Post-Intelligencer*, October 21, 1991, p. C2.

2. Mike Kahn, "Super Sonic," *Sport*, March 1992, p. 90.

3. Glenn Nelson, "Kemp Ages and Rages," *Seattle Times*, November 27, 1991, p. B1.

4. Shawn Powell, "Shawn Kemp is Ready to Create a Sonic Boom," *Basketball Digest*, December 1991, p. 33.

5. Ibid., p. 31

6. Glenn Nelson, "Dial 'M' for Motivated," *Seattle Times*, April 14, 1992, p. C1.

7. Powell, p. 30.

Chapter 6

1. Glenn Nelson, "Straining for Stardom," *Seattle Times*, November 5, 1992, p. E1.

2. Ibid.

3. Ibid.

4. Glenn Nelson, "Kemp's Play Does the Talking," *Seattle Times*, January 21, 1993, p. E1.

5. Associated Press News Wire, June 4, 1993

Chapter 7

1. Glenn Nelson,"Kemp at Eye of Sonic Storm," *Seattle Times*, March 29, 1995, p. C1.

Chapter 8

1. Sarah E. Smith, "Sonics' Time to Shine," *Seattle Times*, November 1, 1995, p. H6.

2. TNT Television, January 19, 1996.

3. Laura Vescey, "Raising His Game," *Seattle Post-Intelligencer*, December 19, 1992, p. D1.

4. Tom Orsborn, "Kemp the New Rage in Seattle" *San Antonio Express-News On-Line*, www.nba.com, February 1996.

5. Vescey, p. D1.

6. Glenn Nelson, "Kemp Displays Trust in His Team," *Seattle Times*, December 3, 1995, p. D12.

7. "Ask the All-Stars," www.nba.com, February 1996.

8. Steve Aschburner, "Kemp's Tip for Garnett is Patience," *Minneapolis StarTribune*, February 10, 1996, p. C5.

9. Bill Knight, "Coming of Age," *Seattle Post-Intelligencer*, November 4, 1993, p. D1.

10. Ibid.

11. Ibid.

Career Statistics

Year	Team	G	FGM	FGA	PCT	FTM	FTA	PCT	REB	PTS	AVG
1989–90	Sonics	81	203	424	.479	117	159	.736	346	525	6.5
1990–91	Sonics	81	462	909	.508	288	436	.661	679	1,214	15.0
1991–92	Sonics	64	362	718	.504	270	361	.748	665	994	15.5
1992–93	Sonics	78	515	1,047	.492	358	503	.712	833	1,388	17.8
1993–94	Sonics	79	533	990	.538	364	491	.741	851	1,431	18.1
1994–95	Sonics	82	545	997	.547	438	585	.749	893	1,530	18.7
1995–96	Sonics	79	526	937	.561	493	664	.742	904	1,550	19.6
1996–97	Sonics	81	526	1,032	.510	452	609	.742	807	1,516	18.7
TOTAL		625	3,672	7,054	.521	2,780	3,808	.730	5,978	10,148	16.2

G—Games Played
FGM—Field Goals Made
FGA—Field Goals Attempted
PCT—Percentage
FTM—Free Throws Made
FTA—Free Throws Attempted
REB—Rebounds
PTS—Points Scored
AVG—Average

Where to Write
Shawn Kemp

Mr. Shawn Kemp
c/o Seattle SuperSonics
190 Queen Anne Avenue North
Seattle, Washington 98109

Index

About the Author

Stew Thornley is an award-winning author and researcher who has written numerous sports books for young readers and adults. He has also co-authored a children's science book with his wife, Brenda Himrich. Stew and Brenda enjoy spending time with their cat, Poncé.